TIME FLIES FOR MS WIZ

Terence Blacker has been a full-time writer since 1983. In addition to the best-selling *Ms Wiz* stories, he has written a number of books for children, including the *Hotshots* series, *The Great Denture Adventure*, *The Transfer*, *The Angel Factory* and *Homebird*.

What the reviewers have said about Ms Wiz:

"Every time I pick up a Ms Wiz, I'm totally spellbound . . . a wonderfully funny and exciting read." *Books for Keeps*

"Hilarious and hysterical." Susan Hill, *Sunday Times*

"Terence Blacker has created a splendid character in the magical Ms Wiz. Enormous fun." *The Scotsman*

"Sparkling zany humour . . . brilliantly funny." *Children's Books of the Year*

Titles in the Ms Wiz series

All *Ms Wiz* titles can be ordered at your local bookshop or are available by post from Book Service by Post (tel: 01624 675137).

Terence Blacker

TIME FLIES FOR
MS WIZ

Illustrated by Tony Ross

MACMILLAN
CHILDREN'S BOOKS

First published 1992 by Picadilly Press Ltd

Young Piper edition published 1993 by Pan Macmillan Children's Books

This edition published 1997 by Macmillan Children's Books
This edition produced 2001 for The Book People Ltd,
Hall Wood Avenue, Haydock, St Helens WA11 9UL

ISBN 0 330 34871 X

7 9 8 6

A CIP catalogue record for this book is available from
the British Library.

Phototypeset by Intype London Ltd
Printed by Mackays of Chatham plc, Chatham, Kent

For Lorraine Boyce and the children of
Wyndcliffe Junior School, Birmingham

ACKNOWLEDGEMENTS

I would like to thank Alice Blacker and Classes 3, 4, 5 and 6 at Allfarthing Primary School, Wandsworth, for helping me with ideas used in this story.

CHAPTER ONE
Jack Beddows is History

"King Henry VIII. Sir Walter Raleigh. Ethelred the Unready . . ." Mr Bailey, the teacher of Class Three at St Barnabas School, called out the names as, his chalk squeaking, he wrote them on the blackboard.

"Who are these guys?" muttered Jack, who was sitting at the back of the class. "Who was Ethel and why wasn't she ready?"

"They're historical characters." Mr Bailey turned to the class, his bushy eyebrows sitting up in what Jack thought of as the Mad March Hare position. "And that's your project for the term – to write about your favourite character in history. You can choose anyone you like. Florence Nightingale, Gunga Din—"

Podge put up his hand. "Can I write something on the man who made the most important invention since time began?" he asked.

"Of course," smiled Mr Bailey. "What did he invent?"

"Chocolate," said Podge. "Thick, creamy, chunky— "

"A serious suggestion, please," said Mr Bailey, raising his voice above the laughter.

There was a long silence in the classroom during which the only

sound that could be heard was the ticking of a clock on the wall. Then, slowly, a hand was raised at the front of the class.

"Sir?" It was Nabila Arshad, the youngest girl in Class Three who had arrived at St Barnabas that term. "My choice will be Joan of Arc."

"Who's that?" muttered Jack. "Noah's wife?"

"She was a young French peasant girl who lived five hundred years ago," said Nabila. "One day she heard

voices telling her to lead the French army against the English, so she became a great soldier."

"Weird," said Katrina. "What happened to her?"

"She was burnt at the stake as a witch."

At that moment there was a faint humming noise from outside the classroom. Puzzled, Mr Bailey looked out of the window. As his back was turned, the children saw a sheet of paper appearing out of thin air in front of the blackboard, then floating down on to the desk.

Mr Bailey returned to his desk and picked up the note. "Why did no one tell me this was here?" he asked, walking quickly to the door. "I have to see the Head Teacher," he said. "I want you all to think about your history project until I get back."

It was shortly after Mr Bailey had left the classroom that Caroline noticed an alarm clock on his desk.

"Strange," she said quietly. "I didn't see that before." She stood up and, having looked out of the window to check that Mr Bailey had crossed the playground on his way to the Head's study, she walked up to the desk. "It's a Mickey Mouse alarm clock," she said.

"Go on, set me then," said Mickey.

Caroline leapt back.

"It . . . it spoke!" she gasped.

The rest of the class gathered around the desk.

"Hurry up," said the clock. "Time waits for no woman."

"I know that voice," said Jack. "And it doesn't belong to Mickey Mouse."

He picked up the clock and carefully moved the alarm button around. Suddenly there was a loud ringing, followed by a puff of smoke – and there, standing by the clock, was a woman in bright blue clothes. She had long dark hair and black nail varnish on her fingernails.

"Ms Wiz!" said Jack. "Of course, it had to be you."

Ms Wiz dusted herself down. "Sorry to give you a fright, Class Three," she said. "I heard someone mention the word 'witch' and thought you might be needing a bit of magic."

"You could help us with our history projects for a start," said Jack. "How can I write about my favourite historical character when I don't know any history?"

Ms Wiz picked up the Mickey Mouse alarm clock. "It just so happens that I have a brand new spell. With this magic timepiece in one hand and an ordinary calculator in the other, I can travel through time. So who'd like to go back in history for their project?"

"Er, I think I'll stick to the library," said Caroline quickly.

"I get travel sick," said Podge.

"There's something on telly tonight that I don't want to miss," said Katrina.

"What about you, Nabila?" asked Ms Wiz.

All heads turned to where Nabila was still sitting at her desk.

"I'd love to go back in time," she said.

"You'll get stuck there," said Podge. "Ms Wiz's spells always seem to go wrong."

"And what about the time I saved the library?" said Ms Wiz. "And the day Herbert the rat climbed up the school inspector's trousers?"

Class Three were so busy remembering Ms Wiz's spells of the past that nobody noticed Jack picking up the Mickey Mouse clock, wandering back to his desk and reaching for his calculator.

That is, nobody noticed, until the alarm on the clock went off.

"Jack!" Ms Wiz shouted – but it was too late. There was the sound of a loud humming noise, followed by a puff of smoke. The clock and the calculator fell to the floor. As the smoke cleared, Jack was nowhere to be seen.

"Oh dear." Ms Wiz had gone quite pale. "We seem to have lost Jack."

"My best friend," said Podge. "Where is he?"

"He must be somewhere in the last five hundred years," said Ms Wiz, picking up the calculator. "Ah," she smiled with relief. "This shows

the numbers 138, which is what we call The Time-Shift Co-efficient. It means—" she tapped some figures on the calculator "—that Jack's in 1854. Or 138 years before that, which is 1716. Or back another 138 years to 1578. Then if you call The Time-Shift Co-efficient 138x and use simple long division—"

"Never mind simple long division!" Podge seemed on the verge of tears. "How are you going to get Jack back?"

Ms Wiz glanced up to see Mr Bailey crossing the playground on his way back from the Head Teacher's study. "Quick," she said. "I need someone to help me fetch Jack. Where's my time-traveller?"

Nabila stood up.

"Ready when you are," she said quietly.

Ms Wiz jabbed a few numbers on Jack's calculator. "We won't be long, Class Three," she said. "And, while we're gone, the clock will stand still, so we'll literally be back in no time."

"What's she talking about?" muttered Podge.

As the door began to open, Ms Wiz handed the calculator to Nabila. The alarm on the clock sounded.

Mr Bailey stood at the door. "Now who—?"

With a puff of smoke, Ms Wiz and Nabila were gone.

CHAPTER TWO
Queen Who?

Travelling through time is not a comfortable experience. It's like being lifted by a great gale and carried through space at incredible speed while all you can see before your eyes is a sort of green minestrone soup. Then, after thirty seconds, the strange, deafening hum in your ears starts to fade as you fall down and down towards the year of your choice to land with a bump.

"Ouch," said Nabila. "My bum."

"Honestly," said a voice behind her. "I take you back four hundred years in time and all you can say is 'Ouch, my bum.'"

"Ms Wiz?" Nabila turned to see a young woman in a brown peasant smock, sitting on the grass beside her.

"You look good," smiled Ms Wiz.

Nabila realised that she too was dressed like a peasant girl. "Four hundred years," she said quietly. "So we have to be in the clothes of the period."

"Jeans would get us noticed," said Ms Wiz, getting to her feet. "Come on, we had better start looking for Jack."

"How do we know he's here?" asked Nabila, following her towards a group of thatched cottages that were nearby. "He could be anywhere in the world."

"If you use the same calculator, you always land in the same place. It's a basic rule of time-travel. By the way, you'll find the calculator in your pocket. Don't lose it or we'll be stuck in 1578 for the rest of our lives."

For the first time, Nabila began to feel nervous. "My mum and dad will be worried about me."

"No they won't," said Ms Wiz. "When we get back to St Barnabas, it will be as if we had only been gone a

few minutes. We've stepped out of time."

"Does that mean we don't exist?"

Ms Wiz stopped. "Yikes, maybe it does," she said, frowning. "You know your trouble, Nabila? You think too much."

"At school, they call me Nabby Know-all. Just because I prefer reading books to running around after a ball."

"I know," said Ms Wiz.

Nabila looked at her curiously.

"What – that the children think I'm odd because I'm so quiet?"

Ms Wiz nodded.

"That—" Nabila looked away, "—that I haven't got any real friends at St Barnabas?"

"But what would happen if you rescued Jack?" said Ms Wiz. "What if you brought him back to the present when all the other children of Class Three had been nervous about a bit of time-travel?"

"I suppose they'd notice me then," said Nabila. "We're not going to get stuck here, are we?"

"And another reason I chose you," said Ms Wiz quickly, ignoring Nabila's question, "is that you can tell me what to expect. For example, what's happening now in 1578?"

"Well, Queen Elizabeth I was on the throne and—"

"Queen Who?" Ms Wiz saw the look of astonishment on Nabila's face. "I'm sorry but at the school I went to, Paranormal Operatives Comprehensive, they only taught things like Spell Technology, Advanced Potion-Making and Practical Magic. We didn't have time for history."

"Actually, I don't know much about Elizabeth," said Nabila. "Except she was very powerful, wore a wig of reddish hair and used to go round saying things like, 'I may have the body of a weak and feeble woman but I have the heart and stomach of a king.' "

"Weak and feeble woman?" Ms Wiz looked shocked. "I don't like that at all."

"It was a long time ago," said Nabila.

As they approached the village, they could see some children chasing a dog that was barking and wagging its tail. A boy of about ten, who had been playing with the other children, looked up and came running towards them.

"Ducking, ducking," he shouted. "Strangers are here for the ducking."

Soon the other children had gathered around. A tall girl with mud in her matted blonde hair touched Nabila's hand. "Why are you so brown?" she asked.

"My parents came from Pakistan," said Nabila.

"Pakistan?" The girl frowned. "That is a funny sounding village."

"Yes, it's just a few miles away," said Ms Wiz quickly. "The sun shines all the year round." She dropped her voice. "I'm going into the village," she said. "You stay here with the children. Ask them if they've seen any children who look like Jack."

"But Ms Wiz—"

"I have to look for someone in the village," said Ms Wiz, turning to the children. "Can Nabila stay with you for a few minutes?"

"Nabila? What a pretty name," said the tall girl. She took Nabila's hand. "I'm Molly. Can you play hopscotch?"

For the ten minutes she was playing with the children, Nabila almost forgot that they were living over four hundred years before she was born. They were just as rough and rowdy as the children of St Barnabas.

"I need to rest," she said eventually.

Molly laughed. "Don't they play

hopscotch in your village?"

"To tell the truth, I prefer reading."

"Reading?" Molly looked puzzled.
"What's that then?"

Nabila shook her head. "Never
mind," she said. "I suppose you
haven't seen a stranger in the village,
have you? He's called Jack."

"There are a couple of Jacks in the
village but I've known them since I
was small. Is this friend from Pakistan
too?"

"No, er – well, near to Pakistan."

"So he'll be brown-skinned too."

"No." Nabila smiled. "He stays indoors a lot."

As they spoke, the sound of voices could be heard coming from the village.

"Come on, then." Molly leapt to her feet. "It's starting."

They followed the other children down a path between the houses, where chickens, pigs and geese wandered free. As they turned into a main street, Nabila saw, gathered in front of the village pond, a crowd of about a hundred people, laughing and jeering. It was only when she and Molly had pushed their way to the front that Nabila saw the reason for their laughter.

A girl of about sixteen was strapped to a chair on the end of a plank, poised over the pond. Through her wild dark hair, her eyes were wide with terror.

"That poor girl," said Nabila. "What are they doing to her?"

"She's no girl," said Molly. "She's P-Peg the Witch. Got the devil in her."

"She doesn't look like a witch to me."

"If you heard her talk, you'd know." Molly laughed. "M-m-my n-n-name's P-Peg. Devil talk."

"She's got a stutter," said Nabila desperately. "It's not her fault."

The cheers grew louder as four of the village men prepared to release the end of the plank that was on dry land. "Duck her!" the villagers were shouting. "Duck the witch!"

At first, Nabila thought that the faint humming sound she heard was in her imagination. Then she could hear the sound of a horse's hooves approaching from the far end of the village. A woman, wearing a small crown on her flaming red hair, was approaching on a magnificent white horse.

There was a gasp from the villagers
as they saw the woman. "The
queen," they whispered to one
another. "It's Her Majesty!"

The woman raised her left hand
and the crowd fell silent.

"My subjects," she cried. "I may
have the body of a weak and—" she
hesitated.

Nabila smiled as she saw who
it was. "The body of a weak and
feeble woman, Ms Wiz," she

whispered under her breath.

"—the body of a weak and fantastically intelligent woman," cried Ms Wiz. "But I have the heart and stomach of a . . . queen!"

There was a gasp from the crowd. "Your Majesty, you honour us with your presence," said a fat, red-faced man, falling to his knees before the white horse.

"Release this girl!" said Ms Wiz. "By order of Queen Elizabeth I."

With quick, panicky gestures, the four men pulled in the plank and untied the girl.

"Come here, my child," Ms Wiz said more gently.

The crowd parted as the girl they had called P-Peg the Witch made her way forward to stand in front of Ms Wiz on her horse.

"If you touch her again, you will be executed. Understand?"

There were murmurs of nervous agreement from the crowd.

"Don't go too far, Ms Wiz," muttered Nabila under her breath.

"Anyway, she isn't a witch," said Ms Wiz on her horse. "She's just got a minor speech deficiency."

"What's she saying?" asked a man near the front. "Sounds like strange talk coming from a queen."

Ms Wiz held up a hand majestically. "Is there a girl called Nabila in this village?" she asked.

Her heart thumping, Nabila made

her way forward until she stood
beside Peg.

"My child," said Ms Wiz. "Give me
the article you have in your smock."

As Nabila fumbled in her pocket
for the calculator, she was aware that
the crowd were growing restless
around her.

"If she's the queen, where are her
soldiers?" the fat man asked loudly.

"Here, that queen's got black
fingernails," said a woman standing
nearby.

"Let's get out of here," Ms Wiz
whispered urgently, taking the clock
from her pocket. "I've never ridden a
horse before in my life."

"But what about Peg?" Nabila
asked. "We can't just leave her."

"Hold her hand!" said Ms Wiz.

As the murmurings from the
villagers grew louder, Peg backed
away from Nabila in fear. "N-n-n-no,"
she said.

Nabila saw that Ms Wiz was

already pressing some numbers on
the calculator. With a desperate lunge,
she grabbed Peg's smock and, with
the other hand, reached for Ms Wiz's
outstretched hand.

"Now, Ms Wiz!" she shouted.
"Now!"

CHAPTER THREE

Russskies in Breeches

It was the noise that Nabila noticed
first. Men shouting, the neighing of
frightened horses, some strange
distant booms. Slowly she opened
her eyes – then snapped them shut.

"Er, no, Ms Wiz," she said quickly,
"I don't think we'll stay here. You
seem to have landed us in the middle
of a war."

Ms Wiz stood up and touched her
silver wig. "It's 1854. I wasn't to
know that there was a war going on
then."

"Hit the calculator!" wailed Nabila.
"If I die in a war that took place a
hundred years before I was born, my
parents will kill me!"

"Nonsense," said Ms Wiz, brushing
down her pink crinoline dress. "This
is just the sort of place we'll find Jack.

That boy seems to attract trouble."

It was now that Nabila looked more closely at Ms Wiz. In spite of her fear, she started laughing.

"This is serious," said Ms Wiz. "War's no joking matter, you know."

"Our clothes," said Nabila, looking at the large golden fan that she was carrying. "People weren't wearing powdered wigs and huge, silly skirts in 1854. We're a hundred years out of date."

Ms Wiz frowned. "Weren't they? I'm sure that I did the right spell."

"Beautiful," said a voice behind them. Nabila turned to see Peg, staring in wonderment at the sky-blue and silver gown she was wearing. "I don't understand," she said in a soft brogue. "What happened?"

"Her stutter," said Nabila. "It's gone."

"Yes." Ms Wiz was fiddling with the Mickey Mouse alarm clock. "Time-travel does that sometimes – it's the shock." There was a faint humming noise, a flash – and Nabila found that she was back in her normal clothes. Ms Wiz and Peg were dressed in T-shirts and jeans.

"That's more comfortable," smiled Ms Wiz.

"We don't exactly look as if we came from 1854," said Nabila.

"Halt!" They heard the sound of cantering hooves behind them as a soldier approached. "Who goes there?" he cried, reining in his horse.

"Only us," said Ms Wiz with a smile. "The thing is, we're looking for a boy called Jack Beddows. He was messing around with my time machine over one hundred and thirty years from now and suddenly – you are listening, aren't you?"

"Ladies?" The man stroked his moustache suspiciously. "Ladies in breeches and odd coloured shirts?"

"Yes, yes." Ms Wiz smiled. "That's what you'll be wearing in the future. At least not you because you won't be around but—"

"*Spies*!" the man shouted suddenly. "Help! Russian spies are upon us! Dressed as ladies in breeches!" He pulled a sword from the scabbard on his belt. "Russkies," he said, pointing the blade at Ms Wiz's throat. "You're under arrest."

"Is this a dream I'm having?" Peg whispered.

Nabila sighed. "I wish it were," she said.

A few minutes later, Ms Wiz, Nabila and Peg were led into a dark, velvet-lined tent. There, seated behind a huge desk on which there was a map, was an older man. In one hand he held a glass of red wine and in the other was a cigar.

"Lord Cardigan, sir!" barked the soldier who had captured them. "I found these three wandering through the camp. They admit to being Russian spies."

"We never!" Nabila burst out. "We just said—"

"Silence!" shouted the soldier.

"Russians?" Lord Cardigan put a monocle to his right eye and peered. "You-ov speak-ov English-ov?"

Ms Wiz sighed. "Your lordship, there has been a terrible misunderstanding." She smiled. "It's

all very simple. We are time-travellers searching for a friend of ours who, we believe, might have landed in 1854."

She took the Mickey Mouse alarm clock out of a bag she was carrying. "Look, this is our time machine."

Lord Cardigan took the clock. "Oh yes," he said, smiling like a little boy who has been given a present. "There's a funny mousey on the front. It's an *excellent* time machine. Thank you very much."

"Careful, sir," said the soldier standing beside them. "It might be a trick."

"It's not a present," said Ms Wiz. "We don't want you zooming through time too, do we?"

Lord Cardigan held on to the clock with both hands. "Mine now," he said.

"Well done, Ms Wiz," muttered Nabila.

"What about you two?" Lord Cardigan turned suddenly to Nabila and Peg. "Are you Russian spies too?" he asked. "Where do you come from?"

"I'm from Class Three at St Barnabas School," said Nabila.

"And I'm a village girl from the reign of Queen Elizabeth I, who's having a very odd dream," said Peg.

Before Lord Cardigan could say anything, another soldier burst into the tent.

"The Russians are about to capture our guns at the end of the valley, sir," he said. "Lord Raglan says we should attack."

"Right!" Lord Cardigan leapt to his feet. "Call up the Light Brigade. We're going to charge."

"No!" Nabila said quickly. "Now I remember what happened in 1854. It was called the Charge of the Light Brigade – you go up the wrong valley and it's all a terrible mistake. I saw a film about it."

"Film? What in deuce's name is a film?"

"You see, sir?" The first soldier barked. "Russian spies, sir. Trying to stop the attack, sir. Given themselves away, sir."

"Quite right." Lord Cardigan was rolling up the map. "Lock them up until we've finished our charge."

"Could we just have our clock back?" said Ms Wiz.

"Funny mousey?" Lord Cardigan looked shocked. "No, he's a prisoner too, aren't you, mousey? Take them away!"

"I think I'd like to wake up now, please," said Peg.

CHAPTER FOUR

The well scared Soldier

Nabila stared into the blackness that was all around her.

"You could have taken us anywhere in history," she sighed. "We could have gone to America just after it was discovered by Christopher Columbus. I could have seen what Pakistan was like in the time of my great-grandparents. But where do we go? To the Crimean War at the Charge of the Light Brigade – which was a disastrous defeat, by the way."

The only sound that came from the darkness was of Peg, sobbing quietly.

"Not that we'll see it since we're stuck here in a prison tent," Nabila continued.

"You don't exactly look on the bright side, do you?" said Ms Wiz at last. "It wasn't my fault that Jack decided to play with my clock."

"He's probably in the Valley of Death by now," said Nabila, gloomily. "You know that poem 'Into the Valley of Death rode the Six Hundred'? It's the Six Hundred and One now. Poor old Jack."

A light flared in front of Ms Wiz, illuminating her face.

"Magic!" Peg gasped.

"Not really," said Ms Wiz. "I brought an electric torch with me." Before Peg could ask what an electric torch was, Ms Wiz added, "Now *this* is magic."

For about a second, the tent was filled with a humming noise. Then Nabila felt as if a great hand had slapped her on the back. When she opened her eyes, she found she was looking at Peg's foot.

'What's happened?" she asked in a voice that was hers, yet more melodic, like that of—

"A bird!" exclaimed Peg. "Nabila had been turned into a little bird."

"Don't worry, Peg," said Ms Wiz. "She'll be Nabila again soon. Disguised as a little bird, she can search the camp for Jack, then bring him back here and rescue us."

"Why me?" said Nabila weakly in her funny bird voice.

Ms Wiz shrugged. "I really wish I could come with you," she said, "but we can't leave Peg alone."

Carefully, she pushed Nabila under the skirt of the tent. "Hurry back," she whispered.

The sunlight blinded Nabila for an instant. Then, seeing two guards at the entrance to the tent, she took a deep breath, spread her wings and began to fly.

Circling high above the encampment, Nabila could see row upon row of English soldiers on their horses, preparing for the Charge of the Light Brigade, but it wasn't at all like the film she had seen. The men looked tired and dirty as they sat on their thin, mudspattered horses. There was no gleam or sparkle to their uniforms. An atmosphere of fear and weariness hung over the hillside.

"Those poor men," thought Nabila as she looked down. "If only I could warn them," she said to herself.

But she couldn't. Ms Wiz had told her that it was a basic rule of time-travel that you're not allowed to change the course of history.

Near one of the tents, she could see a bird coop, on top of which were sitting three pigeons. Flying down, she noticed that the birds had rings on their legs – they were messenger pigeons, used to take notes from one part of the army to the other.

"Any pigeon round here speak English?" said Nabila, hopping onto the ledge beside the pigeons, whose eyes were half-closed. "Any pigeon round here speak anything?"

"Coo," said one of the pigeons.

"Very helpful, I must say," twittered Nabila.

At that moment, she heard from behind a tent, the sound of a man shouting.

"Can't ride? Call yourself a member of the Light Brigade and you can't even ride? Get on that horse at once, you horrible little man – *now!*"

Nabila flew on to one of the guy ropes – and almost fell off with surprise when she saw what was happening beyond the tent.

There, in full uniform but cowering before the biggest horse she had ever seen, was Jack.

"I c-c-can't ride, sergeant," he was saying to a soldier. "I'm well scared of horses."

"Well scared? Well scared?" The man's face was deep scarlet with rage. "What does well scared mean?"

Nabila decided that it was time for action. "It means he won't be going with you," she said as she flew onto the ground near the soldier.

"What?" The soldier whirled around. It took a moment for him to realise that it was a small sparrow that had been speaking to him.

"You're not imagining it," said Nabila, hopping towards him. "I was a perfectly normal person until I was turned into a bird because I used to

shout at people all the time like you're doing. You want to watch out it doesn't happen to you."

The soldier was backing away. "Must be war fever," he muttered to himself. "A bird's talking to me. I'm going mad." He turned and ran in the direction of the other soldiers.

Nabila hopped towards Jack. "If you knew the trouble you've caused us," she said. "We've been looking for you for hundreds of years."

Jack was smiling with relief. "Ms Wiz?"

"Honestly," said the bird. "Do I look like Ms Wiz? I'm Nabila."

"Nabila?"

"Yes, it's Nabby Know-all to the rescue. Now, are you going to follow me or not?"

Jack ran after Nabila as she flew ahead towards the prison tent.

"You keep the guards busy, while I sneak into the tent," said Nabila.

Jack walked up to the two soldiers who were standing at the entrance to the tent. "Is it visiting hour for the prisoners yet?" he asked.

"Visiting hour? What are you talking about?" said the taller of the two guards.

"Hop it, soldier," said the second. "Or we'll—"

He looked around him as a faint humming sound filled the air. Suddenly the guards were enveloped in a puff of smoke. When it cleared, they were standing in white silk leggings, buckled shoes and wigs.

"That is my clothes spell," said a voice coming from the tent behind them. *"If you don't leave us, I'll make sure that you go into the Charge of the Light Brigade stark naked."*

"Wh-what?" said the first soldier, nervously glancing over his shoulder. The other took the wig off his head and looked at it in amazement. "Let's get out of here," he said.

As the guards hurried off, Ms Wiz and Peg emerged from the tent.

"Well done, Nabila," said Ms Wiz to the little sparrow who was perched on her shoulder.

"Hullo," said Jack to Peg. "Where did you come from?"

"It's a long story," said Nabila. "We'll tell you when you get home."

"Why don't we just stay for the battle?" asked Ms Wiz.

"No," said Nabila, a hint of panic in her little bird voice. "I hate violence."

"All right," said Ms Wiz, taking the calculator from the back pocket of her jeans. "Now where did I leave that clock?"

It was Lord Cardigan's proudest moment. He trotted past line after line of his troops as they waited for the order to advance into the valley below. He was thinking of his name in the history books of

the future – the general who
commanded the great Charge of the
Light Brigade.

Behind his saddle was strapped his
newest toy, a timepiece showing the
face of a big-eared mouse. Perhaps, he
thought to himself, it would bring
him luck.

Lord Cardigan was so absorbed in
his thoughts that he ignored the
humming noise coming from the
camp behind him but his horse shied
as if something had touched it. When
he felt behind his saddle, the clock
had gone.

"Mousey?" he said. "Where's
funny mousey gone?"

"Light Brigade ready for action,
sir," one of his officers called out to
him.

At that moment, there was a puff of
smoke from in front of the prison tent
but Lord Cardigan was too busy
spurring his horse forward to notice.

"Charge!" he cried.

CHAPTER FIVE

Just in Time

"—Now who was the joker who sent me to the Head Teacher's office when he wasn't even—?" Mr Bailey stood in the doorway to the classroom, then frowned. At the front of the class, two strangers were standing beside Jack.

"Allow me to introduce myself," said Ms Wiz, stepping forward and shaking Mr Bailey by the hand. "My name's Ms Wiz."

Mr Bailey pulled back his hand as if he had been given an electric shock. "The one with the magic rat? The one who's banned from school for turning a class into pigeons? The one who's always causing trouble round here?"

"Trouble?" Ms Wiz frowned. "I just liven things up a little bit."

"Dare I ask—" Mr Bailey nodded in

the direction of Peg "—who she is?"

"This is my friend, Peg," said Ms Wiz. "She's a bit shocked because she's just travelled four hundred years through time."

"Four hundred years?" Mr Bailey's eyebrows moved into the rare Frightened Pheasants position. "What exactly is going on here?"

"It's all very simple," said Ms Wiz. "Jack got lost in history, so, while you were frozen in time, Nabila and I had to go back to fetch him. We met Peg who was having a bit of a problem back in 1578, then we went to the Crimean War and – oh *no*!"

At that instant, the very same question occurred to everyone in the classroom.

"Where's Nabila?" asked Caroline.

"Ah, problem," said Ms Wiz. "When we left 1854, she wasn't touching me when I made the spell. Still, she should be somewhere nearby."

"Come on, Ms Wiz," said Jack desperately. "It was Nabila who saved me from the Charge of the Light Brigade."

"She was a bird," said Peg quietly.

"Right, that's it," said Mr Bailey firmly. "I'm going to ring the police to tell them a child's been turned into a bird and has gone missing somewhere in the nineteenth century."

"There are some birds in the playground," said Katrina who had been staring out of the window as usual. "The sparrows all seem to be chasing a little bird that's smaller than the rest of them."

"*Do* something, Ms Wiz!" Jack shouted. "That's Nabila and she's getting scragged by a bunch of sparrows!"

Ms Wiz stood by the window. As she stretched out her arms the familiar humming noise filled the classroom. Suddenly, there was

Nabila sitting in the playground. A group of birds that were nearby flew away. She stood up, looked around her, and smiled with relief.

As Nabila walked back into the classroom, the children of Class Three applauded.

"Looks like you're the most popular girl in class today," laughed Ms Wiz.

"Silence!" Mr Bailey banged his desk. "It's all very well travelling through time," he said, "but perhaps Ms Clever Dick Wiz could answer me this question. If she's so magic, why didn't she stop the Charge of the Light Brigade happening?"

"Imagine there was a Private Smith who was killed in the Charge of the Light Brigade," said Ms Wiz. "Imagine that, because magic stopped it happening, he didn't die but came home to marry a young girl from Lambeth. Except the young girl was meant to marry your great-great-grandfather."

"In other words, the whole of history would have been changed and you wouldn't have been born, Mr Bailey," said Nabila.

"Er, really?" Mr Bailey seemed to be trying to work it out in his head.

"Which would have been *really* sad for Class Three," said Podge innocently.

"Right, history project," said Mr Bailey, changing the subject quickly.

"Who's decided on the character they'll be studying?"

"I'm going to read about Lord Cardigan," said Nabila. "I want to know more about the Charge of the Light Brigade."

Ms Wiz stepped forward. "Since she's here, perhaps Peg could tell you all about village life in 1578," she said.

"Yeah, brilliant," said Jack. "Peg could be our favourite historical character. She could tell us all about herself in her own words."

So, for the next ten minutes, Peg talked in a shy voice about her parents, her job as a shepherdess, how it came about that the villagers thought she was a witch because she had a stammer and about the day she was rescued by Ms Wiz and Nabila.

When the bell rang for the end of the lesson, Mr Bailey stood up. "Very interesting, Peg," he said. "Perhaps it's time for Ms Wiz to take you back

to your village." He looked to the
back of the class where Ms Wiz had
been sitting and sighed. "*Now* where's
that woman gone?"

"Look!" Podge pointed at the
blackboard. As if an invisible hand
was holding it, a piece of chalk was
writing a message on the board. It
read:

"HOW TIME FLIES WHEN
YOU'RE HAVING FUN! GOOD
LUCK, PEG. GOODBYE, CLASS

THREE – I'LL SEE YOU THE NEXT
TIME A BIT OF MAGIC'S
NEEDED . . ."

"If Ms Wiz has gone," said Jack,
"who's going to get Peg back to her
village?"

"Perhaps she'd like to stay," said
Caroline.

"And how am I going to explain
her to the Head Teacher!" asked Mr
Bailey. "Sorry, sir, but I've got a
sixteen-year-old girl from
Elizabethan times in my class?"

"I want to go home," said Peg.

Nabila took her by the hand to Mr
Bailey's desk. There, side by side,
were Jack's calculator and the Mickey
Mouse alarm clock. Carefully she
placed Peg's left hand on the clock.
Then she set the calculator to 1578.

"Bye, Peg, take care," she smiled.

"Thank you, Nabila," said Peg.

As her right hand touched the
calculator, there was a humming
sound, then a puff of smoke. The

calculator fell to the ground as Peg and the alarm clock disappeared.

"Wow!" said Lizzie. "Nabila's got magic powers."

"No, that was Ms Wiz magic in the clock," said Nabila.

"Break time, children," Mr Bailey called out.

"Of course," said Jack, "school's a bit boring after you've ridden a huge charger into battle against thousands and thousands of Russians—"

"You were a soldier?" gasped Podge.

It was at that moment that Jack noticed Nabila smiling at him.

"Go on, Jack, this is interesting," she said.

"Well . . . I wasn't exactly *in* the battle," he said. "Maybe Nabila should tell you what really happened."

And the children of Class Three clustered around Nabila as, laughing and asking her questions, they made their way out to the playground.